To Fern and Sofia – R.W.

To Ian and William – C.J.C.

OXFORD
UNIVERSITY PRESS

Great Clarendon Street, Oxford OX2 6DP

Oxford University Press is a department of the University of Oxford.
It furthers the University's objective of excellence in research, scholarship,
and education by publishing worldwide in

Oxford   New York

Auckland   Cape Town   Dar es Salaam   Hong Kong   Karachi
Kuala Lumpur   Madrid   Melbourne   Mexico City   Nairobi
New Delhi   Shanghai   Taipei   Toronto

With offices in

Argentina   Austria   Brazil   Chile   Czech Republic   France   Greece
Guatemala   Hungary   Italy   Japan   Poland   Portugal   Singapore
South Korea   Switzerland   Thailand   Turkey   Ukraine   Vietnam

with associated companies in Berlin Ibadan

Oxford is a registered trade mark of Oxford University Press
in the UK and in certain other countries

Text copyright © 2001 Richard Waring
Illustrations Copyright ©2001 Caroline Jayne Church

Database right Oxford University Press (maker)

First published 2001

British Library Cataloging in Publication Data available

ISBN-13: 978-0-19-272383-3
ISBN-10: 0-19-272383-9

10 9 8 7 6

Printed in China

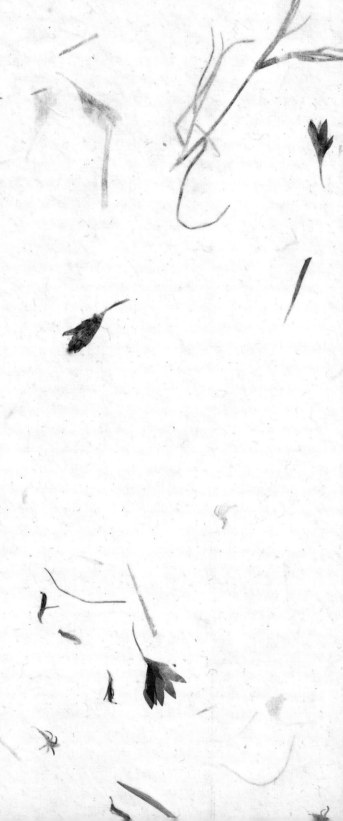

Richard Waring

Hungry Hen

Illustrated by

Caroline Jayne Church

OXFORD

UNIVERSITY PRESS

There was once a very hungry little hen,
and she ate and ate, and grew and grew,
and the more she ate, the more she grew.

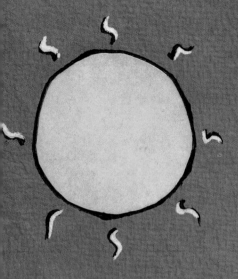

Up on the hill lived a fox.
Every morning the fox stared
down at the farm and the hen
would come out of her coop
looking bigger than ever.

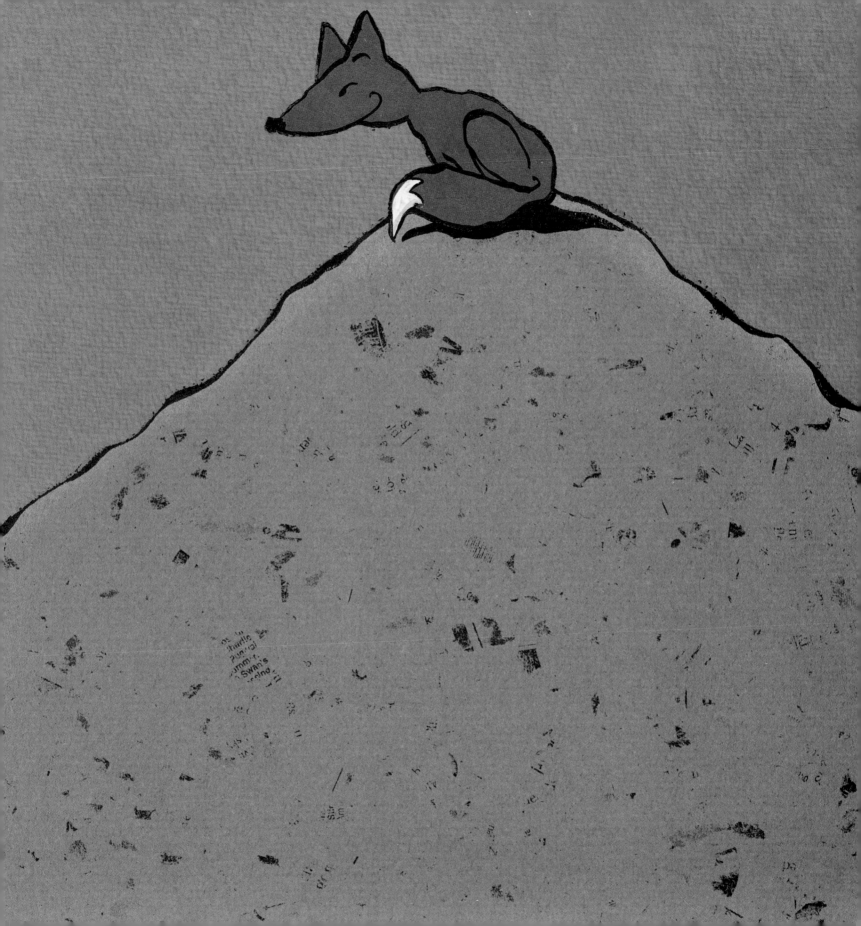

But every morning, as the fox
began to sneak down towards
the farm, he would stop and
think, 'If I wait just one more
day, the hen will be even bigger.'

And so he waited and waited and waited,
and the hen grew bigger and bigger,

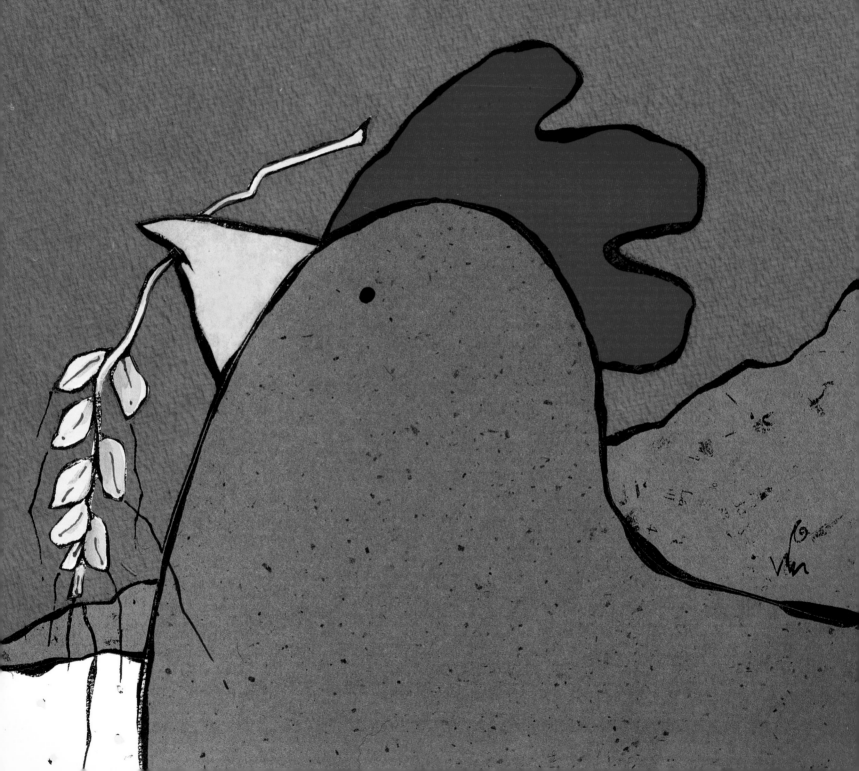

and the fox grew hungrier and hungrier,
and thinner and thinner.

Until one day, the fox looked down at the farm, and all he could see was the hen's enormous head squeezing through the door of her coop.

The fox could stand it no
longer. He began to run.
He ran, and ran.

He ran faster and faster,
straight down the hill,
through the farm,

and crashed through the
window into the hen's hut.

The fox looked at the hen.

The hen looked at the fox.

The fox licked his lips.

And just
as the fox

was about
to pounce...

the hen bent down –
and gobbled him all up!